HIGH SCHOOL MUSICAL

STORIES FROM EAST HIGH #10

TURN UP THE HEAT

TURN UP THE HEAT

By Helen Perelman

Based on the Disney Channel Original Movie
"High School Musical," Written by Peter Barsocchini
Based on "High School Musical 2," Written by Peter Barsocchini
Based on Characters Created by Peter Barsocchini

Disney PRESS

New York

Copyright © 2008 Disney Enterprises, Inc.

All rights reserved. Published by Disney Press, an imprint of
Disney Book Group. No part of this book may be reproduced or transmitted
in any form or by any means, electronic or mechanical, including
photocopying, recording, or by any information storage and retrieval
system, without written permission from the publisher. For information
address Disney Press, 114 Fifth Avenue, New York, New York 10011-5690.

Printed in the United States of America

First Edition
1 3 5 7 9 10 8 6 4 2

Library of Congress Catalog Card Number on file.
ISBN 978-1-4231-0867-2

For more Disney Press fun, visit www.disneybooks.com
Visit DisneyChannel.com

CHAPTER ONE

Gabriella Montez smiled as she walked down one of the long halls of East High. Leaning against her locker was the varsity basketball team captain, Troy Bolton. He was wearing his red-and-white Wildcats jacket and waved at her as she walked toward him. This is the perfect way to start a day, she thought.

"Hey there!" Troy called as Gabriella got closer. "I've been waiting for you. I made this for you." He held out a CD. He'd burned it the night before, after making what he'd hoped would be the perfect playlist. "The first song is by the band I was telling you about."

"Thanks," Gabriella said, touched that Troy had made her a CD. She reached out for the disk. "I can't wait to hear it!"

"Hear what?" Taylor McKessie asked, walking up behind Gabriella.

"Troy heard about this new band from his cousin. They're called The Cooks," Gabriella told her friend. She grinned at Troy, happy that he enjoyed music as much as she did.

"Cool," Taylor said. "The Cooks? Does that CD come with any food? I was running late and didn't get to eat anything this morning."

"Hmm, I wish," Troy replied, rubbing *his* empty stomach. "But these guys just cook up good music, not food."

"Luckily, I'm around, huh?" Zeke Baylor said, appearing before them. He had a large box in his hands. "I made these yesterday. Try one." He held out the open box filled with breakfast buns.

"Zeke!" Gabriella gushed. "You are the best!" She took a bite of the breakfast treat. Between the buttery, flaky crust and the sweet filling, the pastry melted in her mouth. "Yum," she added. "This is amazing."

Troy and Taylor each took a pastry, and then another hand swooped in.

"Can't miss a shot at a Zeke breakfast!" Chad Danforth cried. Then he took a huge bite.

"Did someone say Zeke brought breakfast?" Sharpay Evans asked from across the hall. She noticed that Zeke was holding open a box, and that usually meant a delicious treat. She waltzed over to stand next to him, peering into the box. "Hmm, what do you have there?"

"Oh, these?" Zeke said, trying to be casual about the pastries. "I just whipped these up last night." He turned and offered Sharpay a closer look.

Gabriella watched as Sharpay carefully selected a pastry. It was no secret that Zeke had a crush on Sharpay. And, Gabriella mused, she was sure that Zeke made those pastries with the hope that Sharpay would have one. Sharpay liked the extra attention from Zeke—and the sweets that he gave her. Gabriella was just glad that she got to partake in Zeke's plan to get Sharpay sweet on him!

"Hey, Zeke," Troy said, licking his fingers. "That was really good."

Zeke didn't respond. He was staring straight ahead with his mouth hanging open and his eyes extrawide. "He's . . . he's here," he finally managed to stutter, pointing down the hall.

His friends followed Zeke's finger and saw Principal Matsui walking toward them. Next to their principal was a tall man with jet-black hair, wearing jeans and a chocolate brown leather jacket.

"Who's the dude with Principal Matsui?" Chad asked. He eyed the man walking down the hall. "Nice jacket," he said, nodding in approval at the man's cool-looking leather coat.

"Yes, who is that?" Sharpay asked, pushing

Chad aside to get a better view. "He looks like a movie star."

Zeke spun around to face his friends. "You don't know who that is?" he whispered. He couldn't believe that his friends had no idea that a celebrity was in their school. As his friends stared at him blankly, Zeke explained. "That's Brett Lawrence—one of the best pastry chefs in the whole country. He's the host of *Bake-Off*."

"Hey, I've seen that show," Gabriella said. She glanced at the man next to Principal Matsui. He did look familiar. "It's a fun show," she continued. "Two contestants have to bake something in a short amount of time, using only the ingredients given to them. And he always says, '*Deeeelicious*'!"

"He only says that if he likes the dessert," Zeke corrected. He turned around again to watch as his idol walked down the hall toward him and his friends. There were so many things Zeke wanted to say to the man! He looked down at the empty box in his hands. He couldn't believe that he didn't have one more pastry for Brett to taste.

Just then, Principal Matsui walked up to the group of friends. "Here are some of our students!" he said proudly. "Wildcats, this is Brett Lawrence. He's here to recruit for a special school-spirit-week show that will air on the Baking Channel. It's filming this weekend in Albuquerque and will feature two high school teams. We've just been going over the details of the competition, and it sounds like it will be a fun challenge."

Zeke didn't move—not a muscle. He couldn't speak, either. He had not made one sound since his baking hero had come so close to him.

"We're looking for some East High Wildcats to compete in *Bake-Off* against the West High Knights," Brett said. He glanced around at the students and grinned. "We hope that some of you will participate. We're filming downtown. It'll be a great time."

Sharpay leaned in closer to Brett. "Did you say filming? As in television?"

This was music to Sharpay's ears! A chance to be on television was just too delicious to pass up. She looked at Brett and smiled. "Oh, we can beat West High. Hands down."

"Go Wildcats!" Chad shouted, pumping his fist in the air. His friends cheered.

Troy hit Zeke on the back. "Especially since we have the secret ingredient right here."

Zeke blushed. He had so much to say to Brett, but he was too stunned to utter even one word!

"Well, we're hoping that a lot of students get involved," Principal Matsui said. "We'll tell everyone about the program and all the details in homeroom announcements."

"It will be an exciting show," Brett told the group. "We'll be filming live, asking each team to create a specialty cake in the studio in front of an audience."

"A *live* studio audience?" Sharpay said, batting her eyes. She couldn't believe it! Here was her big chance to make her debut on the small screen and still be onstage with an audience.

"Yes," Brett replied. "Pretty cool, huh?"

"Can we eat the final cakes?" Chad asked.

"You bet!" Brett said. "Hope to see you all on Saturday."

As the principal and the celebrity chef continued to stroll down the hall, Zeke let out a deep sigh. "Wow," he said, still in a hushed voice, "isn't he awesome?"

"That show is going to be amazing," Sharpay said. She had a dreamy look in her eyes. All she could think about was how many doors would open for her once she appeared on the television show. She just had to get on *Bake-Off*.

The first bell for homeroom rang, and everyone started for class. "I'll catch up to you," Zeke called to his friends.

Troy nodded and said, "Sure thing. And hey, thanks for breakfast! Brett will think your baking is awesome." Troy slapped his friend on the back, then hurried off after the rest of the group.

Zeke walked down the hall toward his locker. He felt a little dizzy. He couldn't believe that only moments ago, he'd stood in front of his idol. But Zeke wondered how he was going to impress the celebrity chef if he couldn't even say his name in front of him! His baking would have to speak for itself.

CHAPTER TWO

Sharpay saw her twin brother, Ryan Evans, standing in front of his locker with a stack of books in his arms. "Oh, Ryan," she said, running over to him. "I have the most amazing news!"

Ryan shifted the books to his hip and positioned his red cap on his head. He didn't want to be late for homeroom, but he was curious. "What news is that?" he asked Sharpay.

"Only the most exciting and fantastic news,"

Sharpay told him. Leaning back against the lockers, she hugged her own books close to her chest. "News that we've been waiting to hear *forever*."

Looking at his sister, Ryan's mind raced with possibilities. "We got called back for our dance number for the county variety show?" he asked, full of excitement.

Sharpay's face melted into a frown. "No, not that," she said. "Think bigger." She touched her long, blond hair to make sure it was still in perfect waves.

"Bigger?" Ryan asked. He stared at Sharpay. What was she getting at? Some statewide variety show? Or maybe . . . national?

"Oh, come on! Think!" Sharpay yelled, exasperated.

What was taking Ryan so long to guess? she wondered. She wouldn't be able to wait for him to figure it out at this pace.

"My shot at the big time!" she finally blurted out. "I am going to be the star of a TV show!"

Just at that moment the second bell for homeroom rang, signaling that anyone still in the halls was late. Ryan continued to stare at Sharpay. "What?" he asked. He wondered what had happened from the time they had walked into school together until then. But he'd have to wait until homeroom was over before he got any more information. Sharpay turned before going into their classroom, raised her eyebrows, and smiled. Then she gave her brother a wink.

Ryan shook his head and followed Sharpay into the room. He ducked as he took a seat. Ms. Darbus eyed him for his tardiness and then cleared her throat.

"All right, students," she said to her class. "Please settle down. And pay attention. As always, there are some important announcements this morning. Listen carefully."

The intercom system crackled a bit, and then Principal Matsui's voice bellowed into the classroom.

"Good morning, Wildcats. We have an

important announcement on this Wednesday morning," the principal said. "We have a wonderful opportunity for a group of students to compete in a baking contest for the television show, *Bake-Off*."

Ryan smirked. Was this the big television break that Sharpay had been talking about? Had his sister totally lost it? She didn't even know how to turn on an oven, let alone how to mix cake batter. He eyed Sharpay sitting at her desk across the room, admiring herself in her compact mirror as the announcement was made.

"The competition will be filmed this Saturday with the esteemed chef Brett Lawrence as the host," Principal Matsui continued. "Chef Lawrence is here now to explain more about the show."

"Hello, East High!" the chef said enthusiastically. He had a deep voice, and Ryan could tell he was used to talking into microphones and to large groups of people. "We're looking forward to baked delights produced by the best young chefs when they compete in this Saturday's challenge. The show will have East High competing against West High."

"If you're interested," Principal Matsui said, "see Ms. Davis in the home-economics room to sign up to be part of the East High team. Go Wildcats!"

For the rest of homeroom, Ryan did not listen to any other announcements. He was thinking about his sister's plan. How could she possibly participate in this show? She knew nothing about cooking. In fact, Ryan was pretty sure she'd never baked anything in her life!

When the bell rang, everyone gathered up their books. Ryan met Sharpay out in the hallway.

"See what I mean?" Sharpay gloated. "I'm going to be a television star!"

Ryan stared at his sister. "You're planning on going on this baking show?" he asked.

"Of course!" Sharpay cooed. Her brown eyes were sparkling. She started to walk away. "I know a good opportunity when I see it."

"Sharpay!" Ryan called, catching up to her. "You don't even know the difference between baking soda and baking powder. What makes you think you are going to be part of this team?"

Waving her hand in front of her face, Sharpay dismissed Ryan's foul attitude. "Everyone likes to watch good-looking people on TV. I'll be perfect. Especially with Zeke as the head chef."

"Ahh," Ryan said. Now he understood his sister's master plan. "You're going to get Zeke to do all the work while you strut around the stage."

Flipping her hair back, Sharpay pouted. "Well, clearly I will help, too," she said. "I am a talented person, of course. I can whip butter as well as anyone else." Then she rolled her eyes at Ryan's lack of knowledge. "You know, presentation is a very important part of the dining experience."

"Of course," Ryan said, humoring her. "I am sure that you will make yourself very useful."

"Oh, Ryan!" she cried, not listening to a word

he was saying. "It's just the best news." She began thinking of all she had to take care of before the show. "I have so much to do before Saturday! My hair, my nails." She counted off on her fingers. "And I need to go shopping!"

Ryan watched as his sister headed to her next class. He was happy that she was so excited, but he had to wonder, could Sharpay stand the heat in the kitchen?

Down the hall, Zeke, Gabriella, and Troy walked together to their first-period classes. Zeke was unusually quiet, and he looked like a little kid standing on the edge of the high diving board.

"Hey, bro!" Troy called. "You all set for the big bake-off?"

"Oh, man," Zeke said. "I can't believe this! This is my total dream! You have no idea. Brett Lawrence is my idol!"

Gabriella smiled at Zeke. She wasn't used to seeing him so charged up off the basketball court. Zeke was a huge competitor. Being on the varsity basketball team, he had a drive to win—but this was different. "I wonder who you'll be up against from West High," Gabriella said.

"Doesn't matter," Troy told Zeke. "My boy here is going to win. No problem." Troy gave Zeke a slap on the back.

"Thanks, man," Zeke said. He appreciated the vote of confidence. Suddenly, he started feeling a bit better. He was ready to take the dive. "You guys are going to sign up, right? You'll be part of the team?"

Both Gabriella and Troy nodded. "We're totally on your team, chef," Troy told Zeke.

Zeke smiled. He was glad his friends were going to be there.

"Have you been thinking about what you'll make?" Gabriella asked.

"Maybe something chocolate. My grandma Emma always makes this amazing cake when I visit her in Atlanta. It's really rich and pretty awesome."

"If it's chocolate and you make it, we are

golden!" Troy cheered. "The Wildcats are going to pounce on those West High Knights!"

"What is it about West High that makes everyone go crazy?" Gabriella asked. Still a bit new to East High, she didn't completely understand the whole rivalry with the school across town.

"We've got history," Troy explained. "Our basketball teams have been battling it out on the court for years. And well, Wildcats have a mighty roar."

"Even in the kitchen," Gabriella said with a grin.

"Yeah," Zeke added, smiling. "Definitely in the kitchen!"

CHAPTER THREE

During lunch, everyone in the cafeteria was talking about *Bake-Off*. When Zeke arrived at the table with his tray, his friends were arguing about what designs they thought would be best for the cake competition.

"We are so going to beat West High," Chad said as Zeke sat down at the table.

"Wildcats rule!" their friend and teammate Jason Cross exclaimed, jumping up to high-five Chad.

"I think the cake should have a totally East High look," Chad said. "Like a basketball court complete with nets and balls."

"With a scoreboard that shows the Wildcats up over the Knights," Jason added, reaching over to hit another high five with Chad.

Ryan leaned into the table. He was eager to hear every idea and offer any input he could. He didn't want a West High victory either, so he was very into helping the Wildcats win the challenge. "Maybe it should say something more about all of East High. How about a model of the school?"

"That's a lot of work," Taylor said, shaking her head. She tapped her notebook, which was already filled with drawings and measurements. She and Gabriella were taking detailed notes on everyone's ideas. "You'd have to do everything in the correct proportions."

"No, no!" Chad called out. He nearly jumped out of his seat. "I've got it. We should make a car with actual wheels so that we can roll it into first place."

Zeke dug his fork into his pasta salad. "I don't know, guys," he said. "This all seems kind of hard to pull off."

"Don't worry," Gabriella assured him. "Taylor and I can work up the measurements here on the graph paper so that the cake looks great—and in proportion."

"Not to mention, steady," Taylor added. "Baking is all scientific, you know." She looked around the table. "We'll have to plan out exactly how to build the structure so that it's stable. Our cake won't win if it's fallen to pieces on the floor."

Sitting forward in his chair, Jason voiced his opinion. "Um, I'd just like to remind you all that this is a bake-off, which means the cake not only has to look good, it has to taste good, too."

"Jason's right," Kelsi Nielsen said as she walked over to the table. "If the cake doesn't taste good, it doesn't matter what shape it's in."

Gabriella giggled. "It has to be *deeeelicious*!"

"True, and we definitely need a detailed

plan," Taylor insisted. "You can't just bake a cake and hope that it turns out like what you've imagined."

By this point, Zeke had heard enough. He held up his hands. "Whoa!" he said. "First, the cake is going to taste great. And second, we'll work together to come up with the sweetest Wildcat design."

Taylor couldn't believe how calm Zeke was as he spoke. Was this the same guy who had been paralyzed when he came face to face with Brett Lawrence a couple of hours ago? Something had gotten into Zeke—and Taylor was glad to see it. But she wanted him to be prepared. The pressure of competition could make even the simplest task seem like a challenge. "We're talking national television here," she said to him. She took a bite of her turkey sandwich and glanced around the table for support. "We've got to be the best and present a great-looking cake."

"Exactly," Sharpay said as she walked up to the table.

Taylor turned to her, surprised. She hadn't been expecting to get support from Sharpay, of all people!

"That's where I can be of service," Sharpay continued. She pulled over a chair and squeezed in at the table. She grinned right at Zeke. "You know, I'm a natural in front of the camera. And I'm very good at looking great."

Gabriella and Taylor rolled their eyes, but Zeke didn't seem to mind the attention from his supercrush. Kelsi could see where this was headed and tried to help Zeke refocus.

"Doesn't Brett Lawrence have another saying, 'Dress it up'?" she asked.

"He does," Zeke replied, happy that someone else watched the show. He nodded at Kelsi, appreciating that she had recalled one of Brett's many famous refrains.

"Great decorating *and* taste are both important elements that Brett talks about, but he usually scores higher for taste, doesn't he?" Kelsi asked, facing Zeke. "We need to really concentrate on the cake's smell and flavor, too. Not just what it—or anyone in front of the camera—looks like."

"Brett often says presentation is a key part of the package, though," Zeke added. He was starting to get swept up in the frenzy. If he was going to participate, he wanted to win. He had to make sure Brett noticed who he was and how much he wanted to be an excellent pastry chef.

"I second that!" Sharpay exclaimed, seizing her moment. "Presentation is so important." She flashed a wide grin at Zeke. She could almost feel the lights of the television cameras shining on her already. Sharpay could hardly contain herself. Soon she would be the star of the show, poised to be discovered. No one was going to get in her way.

"Listen," Zeke said to his friends around the table. "Why don't we *all* sign up so we have a strong Wildcats team? It will be fun. With you guys behind me, how can we lose?"

"You got it!" Chad cheered.

Everyone seemed to get whipped up into the baking craze.

"Hey, why doesn't everyone come over tonight so we can watch a couple of episodes of *Bake-Off*?" Zeke asked.

"Like scouting the visiting team!" Chad said. "Maybe there are some subtle hints that we can get from Brett."

Taylor grinned at Chad. "That is such a great idea! Count me in."

Everyone agreed to meet at Zeke's house later that evening. He was happy that his friends were excited about the competition.

"We should also go see Ms. Davis," Taylor said. "I'm sure she wants to get the team started."

"Well, then," Chad said, standing up, "let's get this baking party started." He grabbed Taylor's hand, and they headed for the door. Everyone at the table followed except Zeke and Sharpay.

"Come on, Zeke!" Chad called over his shoulder.

"Are you headed over to Ms. Davis's room to sign up now?" Zeke asked Sharpay.

Sharpay nodded and smiled. "Yes," she said sweetly.

Zeke leaped up. "I'll go with you," he said.

"Oh, brother," Taylor said as she watched them walk away. "This is definitely going to be interesting. . . ."

Ms. Davis happily looked around her home-economics room. She was pleased to see so many students eager to sign up for the baking challenge.

"Please take a seat," she said to the growing crowd of Wildcats. "This is such an exciting opportunity for East High." She beamed at the students. "Brett Lawrence is a wonderful chef, and his special-location show is going to be so much fun!"

Kelsi leaned over to whisper in Gabriella's ear.

"I think Ms. Davis is as excited as Zeke."

"*Almost* as excited," Gabriella teased as she listened to Ms. Davis go on and on about *Bake-Off* and its latest episodes.

"Remember, the final product is not only about presentation, but about taste, too," Ms. Davis said. "So make it *deeeelicious*!" She laughed at her use of Brett's famous phrase.

"See, we told you taste was most important!" Jason called out. He winked at Kelsi, her cheeks reddening as she smiled back.

"I think the best way to handle this competition," Ms. Davis went on, "is to assign a head chef." She focused her eyes on Zeke and smiled. "A head chef is the one who handles the menu, organizes the *sous*-chefs who help prepare the food, and is responsible for the overall presentation."

"Zeke is our man!" Chad cheered.

Everyone in the room hooted and hollered. Zeke was clearly everyone's first choice.

Zeke blushed. Looking down at his hands, he

tried not to be embarrassed by all the attention. He tapped his foot nervously.

"Yes," Ms. Davis said. "I think Zeke is an excellent candidate." She walked over and stood next to him. "Would you like to be the head chef, Zeke?"

Not hesitating one second, Zeke cried, "You bet!" His bashfulness turned into determination. This was what he had dreamed of doing for so long. Sure, he loved baking for his friends and family, but this was a chance to show off his skills like never before.

There was another round of cheers.

"You can all have access to this room for the next two afternoons," Ms. Davis said. "Everyone should go home tonight and think of ideas for the winning cake. Come back tomorrow and talk it over with our head chef." She grinned at Zeke. "Then I suggest you have at least one run-through so that Zeke is comfortable with the timing and recipe. *Bake-Off* is also about strategy. Every moment counts."

After she had finished her announcements, Ms. Davis left the bakers to their task and Troy walked over to Zeke. "Pretty cool, huh?" he asked. "Not only did you get to meet your idol today, you are going to get a chance to bake something for him."

Zeke nodded. He was more than happy about this situation. He looked around the room at his friends. "This is going to be *sweeeet!*" he cried.

He couldn't wait to start planning.

CHAPTER FOUR

On Thursday, Zeke could hardly concentrate in class. After watching three taped episodes of *Bake-Off* with his friends the previous night, he felt as if he could actually picture Brett tasting his cake. And he was psyched! Each period, Zeke watched the clock in the classroom and hoped the minutes would tick by faster. He wanted to get into the kitchen in Ms. Davis's classroom and start baking.

Finally, the last bell of the day rang, and

school was officially over. Zeke headed to Ms. Davis's room with Jason.

"Dude," Chad said, catching up to his friends. "What's cooking?" He had a big smile plastered across his face. While Chad was not as comfortable in the kitchen as on the court, he was totally there for his buddy. "I can't really cook," he admitted as they walked, "but I sure do like to eat!"

"Yeah, man," Jason added. "If you need a taster, I'm your man."

"Plus, I would like nothing better than to beat those West High Knights," Chad said. "They don't have a chance against our man Zeke."

Zeke smiled at his friends. It was great to have his team behind him. He was pretty sure that the taste of Grandma Emma's cake plus a clever design would make a winning combination.

When the boys arrived at the classroom, Gabriella, Troy, and Taylor were already there.

Taylor had her graph paper spread out in front of her on a table. She and Gabriella were ready to draw and calculate the dimensions of any design.

"We're ready if you are," Troy said to Zeke. He wasn't sure what help he could really be, but he was Zeke's number one fan.

Zeke opened his backpack and took out a small white notebook. "I have Grandma Emma's recipe here," he said. "It's been in my family for generations." He tapped the book as he spoke. "I've made this cake dozens of times while visiting her in Atlanta and I think it would be a good base for us to use for the East High cake."

"Sounds good to me," Gabriella said. "Anything chocolate has to be a winner."

"Most people will choose a chocolate dessert over any other," Taylor announced matter-of-factly. She shrugged when her friends all looked at her. "What? I just did a little research on the Internet last night. It doesn't hurt to have facts at your fingertips."

Just then, Kelsi came running into the room. "Hey, you guys," she said, slightly winded. "I just heard from this girl who used to take piano lessons with me. She's on West High's *Bake-Off* team." She took a moment to catch her breath as everyone in the room stared at her.

"What did she say?" Taylor asked, eager to know more about their competition. "Did you find out what they were baking?"

Kelsi shook her head. "Well, no," she admitted. "But I did find out that they have a pretty large baking team. I know Eli Maxwell and Hilary Lloyd are participating."

"Hilary Lloyd?" Sharpay huffed as she entered the room. If there was one name Sharpay didn't like to hear, it was that one. Hilary and Sharpay had both been captains in the Heart to Heart Challenge, an annual Valentine's Day fund-raiser that Sharpay had worked hard on for the United Heart Association. Hilary was also very competitive, and Sharpay looked forward to seeing her lose—again. "Oh, I can't wait to see her face when we take the prize," Sharpay sang out.

"Yes," Kelsi confirmed. "She's definitely on

the team. Apparently, West High is stacking the kitchen with a ton of people." She glanced around the room. "I don't think West High has anyone like Zeke, though. They're pretty nervous about this." She nodded at Zeke.

"Well," Zeke said, rubbing his hands together, "we have a lot of work to do if we are going to make this all look easy."

"Um," Sharpay said, clearing her throat. "Before we begin, could someone please help me out?" She looked around at Troy, Chad, and Jason before her eyes rested on Zeke. "I just need a hand outside for a moment."

Gabriella eyed Sharpay suspiciously. What could she be up to?

Zeke grinned at his crush and rushed out the door behind her. Chad followed out of sheer curiosity. There in the hallway was a large steamer trunk. Ryan was standing next to it with a hand truck. He looked exhausted from pushing the heavy load.

"What is that?" Zeke asked.

"It's all the costume changes I picked out for the show," Sharpay said. "I'm not sure what you are planning on baking, and I want to be able to match the final cake. Colors are *so* important, you know. I want to be sure to sway the vote with the winning combination. I wouldn't want to clash with the cake."

"That's so considerate of you, Sharpay," Chad said, rolling his eyes.

Sharpay disregarded Chad's comment and opened the trunk as if she were opening a closet. She began handing Zeke the outfits she had selected as possible choices for herself.

"That *was* very considerate of you," Zeke remarked, completely genuine. But as Sharpay continued to hand him outfit after outfit, his eyes grew wide. He couldn't believe the number of clothes stuffed into the trunk.

As Chad went back to the classroom to report on the outrageous collection, Sharpay took Zeke's arm and dragged him off to the side. "Whoever helps you onstage is very important,"

Sharpay told him, almost in a whisper. "They'll need to command the audience's attention. Remember, I know all about being onstage."

"You definitely do," Zeke said as he looked down at the red sequined top draped across his arms. "I'm just not sure you'll really need any of these outfits for cooking. Usually chefs wear a white coat and black-and-white checked pants."

"Black-and-white checked pants?" Sharpay's voice cracked. She looked horrified at the fashion choice of chefs. What were they thinking?

Zeke nodded meekly. "Or they wear an apron," he said. "A kitchen can get pretty messy." He held out the sequined top. "This could get ruined really quickly."

"Hmm," Sharpay said. Then her eyes grew wide. "Wait, are you saying this because you are going to pick me to be onstage with you?" She held her breath as she looked into Zeke's eyes. She could only hope that her plan was going to unfold just as she had imagined.

Without a word, Zeke walked back to the

trunk and placed the costumes inside. "Let's get started," he said and waved Ryan and Sharpay into Ms. Davis's room. "We don't have that much time."

Sharpay turned to give Ryan a wink and then followed Zeke. How could Ryan have doubted her plan? Clearly, Zeke was going to ask for her assistance. He may have required a little help realizing that he needed her, but Sharpay was more than willing to give him a gentle nudge. She wasn't exactly sure what a *sous*-chef did, but as long as it meant standing in front of a camera, then she was all for playing the role.

Zeke glanced around the room at his friends. "I want you to know that I'll need all of you to help me plan everything out," he said. "But onstage, I think it will be best to just have one *sous*-chef to assist me."

Sharpay held her breath. She had to be the person Zeke wanted up on the stage. She just had to be!

Shaking his head, Ryan stood at the door. He

was anxious to hear what Zeke was about to say. Sure enough, he thought, the girl who has never boiled water has probably talked her way into being a *sous*-chef.

Zeke cleared his throat and announced, "Sharpay, you'll be right next to me, handing me ingredients and making sure we stay on schedule." He looked right at her and loved seeing her stare back at him.

"So I'm your *sous*-chef?" she asked, her brown eyes sparkling.

Zeke couldn't have been happier. "Yes," he confirmed to the shock of everyone else in the room. Sharpay squealed with glee.

As preparations got underway, Gabriella watched Zeke show Sharpay how to use a flour sifter. She had to stifle a laugh. Was he really explaining how to sift flour to her? No matter how great a performer she was, Gabriella thought, how was Sharpay going to fake being able to cook? Zeke's crush had definitely blinded him. How could Sharpay help Zeke bake when all she cared about was where the camera was and if she was in its frame? Gabriella sighed. She wanted to win just like everyone else at East High, but with Zeke's choice for his *sous*-chef, she wondered if they'd stirred up a recipe for disaster.

CHAPTER FIVE

"**T**GIF!" Troy cheered as he entered Ms. Davis's classroom after school that Friday. The home-economics room smelled like banana bread, probably from the last period's class. Ms. Davis wasn't in the room, but on the blackboard she'd left the baking team a message: GOOD LUCK, CHEF ZEKE AND TEAM! GO WILDCATS!

"You got that right!" Chad yelled back, looking up at Troy. Chad and Jason were already sitting at one of the long tables. They were hovering over one of Taylor's charts, plotting the East High cake design.

"This weekend is going to rock," Chad went on. "We're going to come out on top Saturday."

"West High is going to have egg on their faces, that's for sure," Jason added.

"Totally," Troy said. He peered over their shoulders. "The Wildcats design that Taylor and Gabriella came up with is awesome."

"I don't know," Chad said. He took the paper into his hands to examine it more closely. "I still think that we should go for something flashier . . . and taller."

"You should talk with the head chef about that," Troy said. He put his backpack on the ground and pulled up a stool next to his friends. "I don't think he liked their design choice either. Knowing Zeke, he probably has another idea up his sleeve."

"Oh, Zeke's not here yet?" Kelsi asked as she raced into the room.

"He's coming," Chad said. "Don't worry. He

just went to the store to get some ingredients."

"I thought I was going to be late," Kelsi said, relieved. She dragged a stool over to the table where they were sitting. Kelsi was looking forward to seeing—and tasting—Zeke's creation. Today, the team planned to take Ms. Davis's advice and time their test run. Plus, it was important for everyone to taste the cake!

"Did we decide on a design?" Kelsi asked. She wasn't sure how things had ended up the day before. Soon after Zeke told Sharpay that she could be his *sous*-chef, everyone had left.

"Well, Taylor thinks it's going to be a Wildcat leaping through a basketball net," Chad said, holding up the paper. "But Zeke isn't here yet, so it's hard to say what he'll do."

Just then, Zeke walked in holding two large grocery bags. Sharpay and Ryan trailed behind him.

"Hello, Wildcats!" Sharpay sang as she paraded into the room. "Wait until you see what I've got in my bag!" she squealed as she pulled out a bright red apron that glittered with red-and-white rhinestones. It was blinding.

"Wow," Troy said. "That's definitely some school spirit."

"And very sparkly," Kelsi added.

"Go Wildcats," Chad said softly, trying to stifle a giggle.

Sharpay put on the apron and placed her hands on her hips. She was sure the apron would be a stellar hit. Red looked great on her, and the camera loved bright colors. "Ready to bake!" she cried, smiling and waving to the group.

Troy noticed that Zeke didn't even look up at Sharpay. He was busy pulling all the ingredients out of the bags and setting them up on one of the tables.

"Hey, where are Taylor and Gabriella?" Jason asked.

"They have a Scholastic Decathlon meeting," Troy told him. "But they'll be here later. They wouldn't miss the trial run."

Zeke carefully looked around his workstation.

He had lined up the ingredients in the order he would need them. He wanted his timing to be perfect. "Okay," he said to the group, "let's get this party started!"

Kelsi took out a large stopwatch. "I'll keep time for you, Zeke," she said. "If you're ready, I'll start the timer."

"Wait!" Chad called as he pushed a rolling cart with a microwave on top. He positioned the cart right in front of Zeke's table. "Let's say that this is the camera. If this is a run-through, then we should make this as much like the studio as possible."

Sharpay nodded eagerly. She was all for practicing her performance in front of an audience—and a camera. She faced the microwave and waved.

"Jason and I can't stay, though," Chad said. "We promised Coach Bolton that we'd help clean out the equipment room."

"Yeah, but we'll be back to taste the cake when it's done," Jason told Zeke. "Can't wait!"

"Sure," Zeke said, not really paying attention. Opening his little white notebook, he read over the recipe one more time. He took a deep breath and looked at Kelsi. "Okay. Go!" he called, signaling her to start the timer. He dug a measuring cup into the flour bag and dumped it into the sifter. "Sharpay, sift the flour into this bowl. Then add the baking powder." He handed her the large bowl. "Then start the mixer to cream the butter with one cup of sugar." He clapped his hands together and went over to grate the bittersweet chocolate.

"You know," Kelsi said from her stool, "I was reading last night that if you add some chili powder to chocolate cake, it adds a bit of kick. Maybe we should try some?"

Zeke raised an eyebrow. "Hmm," he said. He grabbed some eggs. "Maybe."

Kelsi shrugged. She wasn't too sure of herself in the kitchen. If this were a music competition, then she would have been much more confident. She was looking for ways to set the Wildcats apart from the competition, though; she, too, was getting into the rivalry against West High and wanted to win. But at Zeke's dismissal, she settled back on her stool and watched the run-through.

Still standing front and center, Sharpay was busy smiling for the makeshift camera. She had barely sifted the flour, and she had not even gone near the mixer.

"Sharpay!" Zeke called. "You didn't turn on the mixer yet!"

Running over to the machine without turning her back to the "camera," Sharpay grinned sheepishly at Zeke. "Oh, well . . . er . . . I . . ." she stuttered.

She ran her hands over the mixer. How do you turn this on? she wondered.

"I'll get it," Zeke mumbled. He reached over her and flipped the switch on the side. "Just put the sugar in there and hand it to me when it's all creamed."

Rolling his eyes, Ryan gave Kelsi a gentle nudge.

"This isn't going to be good," he whispered.

"You got that right," Kelsi murmured back.

With a smile glued on her face, Sharpay handed the mixing bowl to Zeke. She was rather pleased with herself. What was so hard about baking? She tossed her hair and waited for her next instructions like a good actress awaiting her next stage direction. "Here you go, chef," she said sweetly.

When Zeke looked in the bowl, something seemed off to him. The color and consistency were wrong. He dipped a spoon into the bowl and tasted the mixture. Immediately, he made a sour face. "SHARPAY!" he screamed. "I said a cup of *sugar*, not salt! Don't you know the difference between them?"

Horrified, Sharpay quickly picked up the bag that she had dipped the measuring cup into. There was another bag right next to it. Both bags were white and both had grainy white substances inside them. It's an innocent mistake, right? she thought. But she had never heard Zeke so angry. Holding up her hands, she tried to appeal to him. "Oops," she said.

Zeke paced in a circle and didn't say a word. He gripped his hands in tight fists. Finally, he took a deep breath and went over to grab Troy's arm. He pulled him out into the hallway. "You've got to help me!" he pleaded. "Sharpay is driving me nuts. All day, she has been showing me different aprons and outfits. She's gonna blow this competition for me before it even starts!"

"What can I do?" Troy asked, trying to be a good friend.

"Please be my second *sous*-chef," he begged. "All you have to do is keep Sharpay busy—and away from the food. I'll do the rest."

Troy raised his eyebrows. Controlling Sharpay was not an easy task, but he knew how much this competition meant to Zeke. He had to help him out. "I've got your back, buddy," Troy told him. As soon as Troy walked back to the table, he grabbed the mixing bowl and handed it to Sharpay.

"Why don't you clean that out over there?" Troy said, directing Sharpay over to the sink at the end of the long table. "I'll help you."

Sharpay giggled. Obviously, Troy was feeling left out. She had to hand it to herself. She knew that her plan to be Zeke's *sous*-chef was a good one, but she had not counted on the extra attention from Troy as well. What a delicious bonus!

"Troy is going to be my second *sous*-chef," Zeke announced. Then he turned to Kelsi. "Just take about three minutes off the final time to make up for that . . . delay. Okay?" Kelsi nodded, and Zeke went back to work, separating the egg yolks from the whites.

Thinking of jobs for Sharpay to do while Zeke made the cake was not easy, but Troy stayed true to his word and kept her out of the way. Sharpay was so busy feeling admired as the star of the kitchen that she didn't seem to notice.

A while later, Gabriella and Taylor walked into Ms. Davis's classroom. A warm, delicious chocolate-cake scent filled the air.

"It smells really good in here," Taylor said.

"The cake's almost done . . ." Kelsi told them, checking her stopwatch. ". . . with plenty of time to spare. Zeke has been amazing."

It wasn't hard to miss Sharpay with her rhinestone apron and giddy laugh. Gabriella saw her drying off a bunch of mixing bowls with Troy at her side. Sharpay kept touching Troy's arm and tossing her hair around like she was in a shampoo commercial.

"What's all this?" Gabriella whispered to Kelsi, nodding in their direction.

Kelsi sighed. "I think that's Troy's way of helping Zeke. He's keeping the glamour-girl *sous*-chef away from the food!"

Just then, the buzzer on the oven rang, and Zeke raced over to get the cake. He put on the large oven mitts and pulled it out.

"Oh, no!" he cried when he saw the cake.

In Zeke's hands was the flattest-looking

pancake that he'd ever seen. It looked nothing like Grandma Emma's cake.

"Is it a chocolate crêpe?" Sharpay asked. "How French!"

"No!" Zeke barked. "It's a total failure."

CHAPTER SIX

"Yo, where's the cake par-tay!" Chad yelled as he and Jason danced into the home-economics room. After all the equipment-room cleaning, they were ready for a supersugary snack.

"Give me some of that chocolate magic!" Jason sang out. But when he saw the stunned faces of his friends, he got really quiet. This was not the scene that he had anticipated.

"Um, what's up, guys?" Chad asked, looking

to Troy for an explanation. He had expected to see a bunch of happy, cake-eating people in the room, not a silent group of mourners. He looked around. No one was holding plates or forks. "Where's the cake?"

Troy nodded to the pan cooling on the table in front of Zeke. "The cake's a little flat . . ." he started to explain.

"Not to worry," Jason chirped, moving closer to take a look. "Let's have a taste." He grabbed a fork from the table and reached out for a bite. No matter what the shape, Jason wanted to try some of the dessert.

"Oh, no," Troy said, blocking Jason's lunge. "You can't taste the cake yet. We still have to put on the icing and decorate it. I'm the new *sous-chef* around here," he said, sticking out his chest proudly. "And the cake is not ready yet."

"All right," Jason said, backing off. He raised his arms as if he were surrendering. Then he smiled and bowed, sweeping one arm out to offer Troy some room. "Well then, let's see you work." He backed up and sat down on one of the stools to watch. Troy was one of the greatest basketball players at East High, but he wasn't really known for his baking abilities. Jason was all for Troy giving it a try—especially if it meant he got to have some chocolate cake sooner rather than later!

Over at the table, Zeke was shaking his head as he stared at the flat cake. "I just don't understand," he mumbled. He looked over his recipe very carefully. "We did all the right steps." He looked at the ingredients on the table. Then he paused. There was just one part of the recipe that he didn't witness happening. And it was pretty important. "Wait," he said, thinking out loud. "Sharpay, did you put in the baking powder after you sifted the flour?"

"Huh?" Sharpay asked. She was busy dusting off the flour from her apron on the other side of the room. The flour was making her rhinestones dull, and she wanted them to maintain their maximum amount of sparkle. She was thinking hard about a plan for Saturday, too—she didn't want to lose her shine in front of the cameras! "What was that, Zeke?" she called sweetly.

"Did you put in the baking powder?" Zeke said again, trying not to raise his voice. He clutched his hands and took a deep breath.

Sharpay crossed the room to stand next to Zeke. "Baking what?" she said, pouting and widening her eyes.

"The baking powder!" Zeke exploded. He lifted up the container and shook it at her. "How could you forget that? You were supposed to put a teaspoon of it into the sifted flour!" He rubbed his hands over his face, leaving a smudge of flour on his forehead. "No wonder the cake is flat," he grumbled.

How could he even attempt to impress Brett Lawrence if he couldn't get his cake to rise? Suddenly, this competition had changed—what was once a wonderful dream had become a total nightmare!

Sharpay stood still, too stunned to speak. Zeke

had never spoken to her that way before. She thought that she was being a fantastic *sous*-chef. She had a winning smile and a dazzling apron, after all.

Feeling bad about yelling, Zeke took a long look at Sharpay. She looked so cute in her team-spirit apron. He shook his head; it was all his fault. The *sous*-chef only follows the head chef's directions, Zeke reasoned. Maybe he just hadn't been clear enough. "I'm sorry, Sharpay," Zeke said softly.

"Chemistry," Taylor mused from across the room. She stood up from her stool and walked over to Zeke as if she were a detective on a tough case. She loved seeing how applications of science seeped into daily life. And more than that, she loved to point out interesting facts to people. "See, this is a good example of science at work. You need the baking powder to make the cake rise. It's actually amazing that just a little bit can do it." She stopped and picked up Zeke's recipe notebook. Staring at the recipe for a moment, she tapped her finger on her chin. "But there also might be another problem here. . . ."

Before Taylor could continue, Ms. Davis opened the door and walked in. "Hello!" she sang out happily. She sniffed the air. "It smells good in here." She flashed a smile at Zeke. "How is everything going, chef?"

"Not very good," Zeke mumbled. He pointed at his cake. "We didn't add the baking powder, so it's a bit flat." Now he was even more upset with himself because he hadn't checked to make sure the most important ingredient had been added. After all, he was the head chef and there-fore responsible for everything that happened in the kitchen. He had heard that many times on *Bake-Off*, during the critique at the end. Brett often had to reprimand the chef for not guiding his or her team more carefully.

"Ah, I see," Ms. Davis said slowly. She nodded in agreement as she surveyed the cake. "Well, that is what a run-through is for. Better to have this happen today than tomorrow at the competition. Now you have some time to figure out what went wrong and make some adjustments."

Ryan popped up out of his seat and put a hand on Zeke's arm. "You know, Ms. Darbus always says that a bad dress rehearsal means a great show!"

"I'd have to agree with that," Ms. Davis remarked. She gave Zeke an encouraging smile. "Don't worry. Why don't you take the time now to perfect the decoration? You only have about twenty minutes left here in the room. Once the janitor comes to clean, you'll have to leave." She turned toward the door. "Good luck, and I'll see you tomorrow at the studio!"

When Ms. Davis left, Troy could tell that Zeke was not focusing on anything except his flat cake. As his second *sous*-chef, Troy felt that he had to help. The only thing was, he wasn't sure what he could do.

Suddenly, Sharpay's cell phone rang. She flipped it open. "Helloooo," she said. Her face quickly formed a pout as if she had just eaten a sour-lemon drop. "Uh-huh," she said through gritted teeth. "Well, we'll see about that," she growled. She looked at Ryan and mouthed, "Hilary Lloyd." She paced around the room, listening intently and then said, "Okay, well, we'll see you tomorrow."

"Did she tell you what West High is baking?" Jason asked when Sharpay closed her phone.

"It doesn't really matter," Zeke said with a groan. "If we can't even get this cake to rise, there is no hope for us. Plus, this frosting is just not working." He lifted his spoon up for everyone to see. "It's supposed to be smooth, not lumpy with crunchy sugar pieces."

Taylor walked over to inspect the icing. "Wow," she said. "You see, I think that—"

"Hello?" Sharpay called out, interrupting Taylor. "Doesn't anyone want to know what Hilary told me? I think I have some valuable information here!"

Everyone turned to look at Sharpay. She took

in the moment, enjoying everyone staring at her. "Well," she said, "West High has ten people who will be working onstage tomorrow. Hilary wouldn't tell me what they were baking, but she was bragging about ten layers."

"Ten layers!" Jason cried. "That sounds hard to beat."

"Jason!" Gabriella snapped, giving him a gentle slap. "More isn't always better."

"Ah, but height is good," Chad said, feeling like no one had been paying attention to his idea of a taller presentation.

"Remember that episode from Texas that we watched at Zeke's house the other night?" Kelsi asked.

"Yeah," Ryan said. "Brett kept talking a lot about building up the dessert."

"See?" Chad said. "The man likes some flash."

"But it's about the taste, too," Gabriella piped up. "Brett also says, 'Looking good, tasting good'."

It made Troy smile to hear everyone quoting

Brett Lawrence. Just a few days earlier, most of them hadn't even known who he was, let alone what he thought of desserts. He saw Zeke slumped over on his stool. He must be really bummed out about the cake, Troy thought. "Maybe we should do the decorating part now and see how the 'Wildcat' turns out," he suggested.

"Awesome!" Jason cried. "Because I was thinking that we should try some of these red candies." He held up a box of cinnamon candies for Zeke to see. He smiled, thinking that Zeke was going to love his idea.

"Or why not cut the cake in half and make at least two layers?" Chad said. "Or even better, four layers!"

"But I really think that we need to—" Taylor didn't get a chance to finish her thought because Zeke had finally hit his boiling point.

"Stop!" Zeke screamed at the top of his lungs. His face was getter hotter and hotter, and the oven was off! He couldn't take all the cooks in the kitchen anymore. If he was going to be responsible for the Wildcats' cake, then he was going to do it his way. "That's it!" he bellowed. "No more!"

Everyone turned to look at him.

"Tomorrow," he said, "I bake alone!"

CHAPTER SEVEN

Gabriella shivered and zipped up her red Wildcats sweatshirt. "It's so cold in here," she said to Taylor, who was sitting next to her on the bleacher seats overlooking the *Bake-Off* kitchen. In the studio, there were two fully-equipped kitchens next to each other, with a long, white judges' table set up in between them. The television studio felt as cold as a freezer, and Gabriella dug her hands into her pockets to keep them warm.

"I know," Taylor said. "My teeth are chattering!"

Kelsi, who was sitting in the row in front of Gabriella and Taylor, turned around. "I read in a magazine that Brett Lawrence likes it that way, and he actually demands that the *Bake-Off* studio be this cold." She smiled as she went on. "He might be a great chef, but he is definitely a prima donna!"

"Talk about prima donnas," Taylor mumbled. She nodded down to the kitchen where Zeke was busy getting his ingredients in order. "I wish he had talked to us this morning or last night. We could have helped him. This is going to be hard to watch."

Gabriella nodded in agreement. They had done some research the night before and come up with a few adjustments for Zeke to make to his chocolate cake. They had left messages for him on his cell phone and tried to get his attention when they all arrived at the studio, but Zeke hadn't wanted to discuss his plan.

"Go, Knights!" a loud team chorus rang throughout the studio. A lineup of ten West High students jogged onstage to their television kitchen. Each one was wearing a chef's hat with a Knights logo and matching T-shirt. Eli Maxwell, the head chef, led the team around the kitchen as they cheered.

"Just look at Hilary," Sharpay grumbled to Ryan as she viewed the scene from her seat. She was seething because Hilary was going to be on camera for the show while she would be seated in the audience. I should be onstage, Sharpay thought bitterly. This was supposed to be my big break!

"Hey, Wildcats!" Troy called out. He climbed up the bleachers to sit next to Gabriella. Jason and Chad were right behind him. "Anyone talk to Zeke today?" Troy asked.

"No," Gabriella answered. "And Taylor and I have some information that would really help him."

Troy shook his head. He knew that Zeke was set on doing this competition alone, but he also knew that teamwork was the way to win.

"We tried again this morning," Chad said. "He wants nothing to do with us."

"He's definitely upset," Jason added. "I haven't seen him this burned since he missed those two foul shots against West High last year."

"Maybe we should try again—right now, before the show starts," Troy suggested. He watched as Zeke paced around the kitchen.

"That's exactly what I was thinking!" Gabriella exclaimed. She loved knowing that she and Troy were on the same page. Reaching out to grab his hand, she smiled at him. "Let's walk down there and try to get Zeke to listen."

"Ladies and gentlemen, we'll begin in just thirty seconds!" a voice boomed through a microphone. The house lights dimmed, and large floodlights lit up the kitchen set.

"I guess we just missed our chance," Troy said, sitting back down with a sigh.

Gabriella looked concerned. "Poor Zeke," she whispered. "He's all by himself."

A few rows down, Sharpay bit her finger so she wouldn't scream. She was so close, yet so far from those television cameras. It was almost too hard to sit still.

"Welcome to *Bake-Off*! Today, we're broadcasting from Albuquerque, New Mexico, for a special, school-spirit-week show! Our two high school teams competing today are the East High Wildcats and the West High Knights," the announcer trumpeted. The audience burst into applause.

Gabriella saw that Troy was worried. Unlike at a basketball game, he wasn't center court with Zeke. She could tell that he felt badly about Zeke playing solo. She took his hand. "Maybe things will work out better than we think," she said brightly.

Raising his eyebrows, Troy looked skeptical, but he squeezed Gabriella's hand. Maybe she's right, he thought. Maybe this won't be a total mess.

The announcer was now introducing the

judges of the show as a spotlight hit the long white table. "We're so happy to have Liz Warren, Albuquerque's most respected food critic. Please give her a warm welcome!" A woman with long red hair stood up and waved to the crowd.

"She can be pretty harsh," Kelsi leaned back to whisper to Gabriella. "I remember her review of a new seafood restaurant where she said the kitchen probably couldn't make anything that tasted better than frozen fish sticks. And her review about a French restaurant that wasn't even capable of making French toast. She's tough."

"Poor Zeke!" Gabriella said again, nervous for her friend.

"And we're very lucky to have the famed Jacques Milleux," the announcer went on. "He trained in France and has lived all over the world. He is the owner of La Mer here in Albuquerque and is one of the finest chefs in the world."

The audience cheered and settled down in their seats to wait for the show to begin. Brett

Lawrence got up and took the microphone from the announcer. He welcomed everyone, and then he pointed to the large clock behind him. "This is the official time clock. The contestants' cakes must be completed before time runs out," he told the audience. "And *Bake-Off* officially starts *now*!"

Eli and his West High Knights sprang into action. Even though there were a lot of them in the small space, they all seemed to be working together like a well-oiled machine.

Looking over at the crowded Knights kitchen, Zeke wished that his friends were next to him and not somewhere in the bleachers, hidden by the bright stage lights. He turned around and saw Brett staring at him, and he quickly got his game back on. Zeke might have been paralyzed the first time he met him, but he wasn't now. This was his big chance, and he wasn't going to blow it. And he wouldn't forget a single ingredient this time.

"Look at him move," Chad commented as he

watched Zeke. He was impressed with Zeke's speed as he whipped around the set. "He is a man on a mission, that's for sure."

In the front row, Sharpay turned to Ryan. "I can't just sit here like this!" she cried. "Look how Hilary keeps smiling for the camera. It should be me up there, I tell you!"

Ryan patted his sister's knee. "Easy there, chef," he said. "Just be patient. If Zeke wins, then all of the Wildcats will be on camera."

Ah, thought Sharpay, a victory shot of all the adoring fans. She watched the clock with renewed enthusiasm, waiting for Zeke to finish and to be crowned the winner—or so she hoped.

Zeke's timing was just as he had calculated. He looked over at the West High kitchen where there were people scurrying around like buzzing bees. Because he didn't have all those people the way Eli did, he was able to be more efficient. He was already putting his cake in the oven. It didn't seem as if the Knights were anywhere near cooking time. Zeke was pleased. This meant that he had more time to concentrate on his icing and decorating.

When the buzzer on the oven rang, Zeke held his breath as he opened the door. He hoped the cake had not fallen flat. He carefully slid it out of the oven and onto the cooling rack. When he looked down at his cake, he let out a huge sigh of relief. The cake was flatter than he would have liked, but it was better than yesterday. A roar was heard from the crowd—a Wildcats roar. Zeke was psyched that his friends were all there and still cheering him on. He had been really harsh on them, he thought. It felt good knowing that they were rooting for him now.

He glanced over at West High as they bickered over which pans to use for the batter. Then he took his icing, which was still a bit lumpy, and started to build the cake.

As Zeke layered the cake, Taylor leaned over to Gabriella. "I can't watch," she whispered. "Knowing what we found out last night, this is going to be bad."

"I know," Gabriella said. "But let's try to think positively. It is looking pretty good."

When Zeke had finished, the cake was six layers high. It looked fantastic. It wasn't shaped like a Wildcat, but it had the school colors boldly striped across the top. Zeke even had a ton of time to spare! No one could believe it.

According to the rules of the competition, the finished cakes had to be displayed on the judges' table. Zeke carefully slid the tray holding his masterpiece off the counter of his workstation and headed for the table. He walked slowly, keeping the cake steady in his hands.

Kelsi turned around to look at Gabriella and Taylor. "What do you think?" she whispered. "Maybe the cake is okay after all?"

Gabriella and Taylor exchanged nervous glances. They'd filled Kelsi in on what they had discovered the night before. They hoped she was right, but . . .

"Oh, no!" Taylor gasped at the same time Gabriella's mouth dropped open in a horrified 'O.'

Kelsi spun around just in time to see the cake start to wobble in Zeke's hands. Then, just as Taylor had feared, one side of the cake began to slide. All six meticulously decorated layers collapsed into a gooey mess of chocolate and red-and-white icing. The cake oozed off the platter and onto the floor—right in front of the judges' table.

The studio fell silent. The East High students looked on in horror, while the West High students were caught between shock and triumph. As bad as they felt for their competitor, the Knights couldn't help but think that this guaranteed their win.

Gabriella cringed and Taylor dropped her head into her hands. This was worse than they'd expected. They wished they could help Zeke, but they didn't know how.

CHAPTER EIGHT

Zeke froze. He didn't want to look up and see Brett's expression—or any of the other judges' faces. How was he supposed to present his layered cake, which was now just a sloppy mess? He had not only ruined his dream of baking for his idol, but he had also embarrassed himself. And he had let down all the Wildcats who had believed in him.

"There's still time, don't give up!" a voice called.

It was music to Zeke's ears. He looked up and saw Sharpay standing by her seat in the front row, cheering him on. She was wearing a Wildcats sweatshirt. This clothing didn't have any rhinestones on it, but her smile was as sparkly as ever. Zeke got a rush of new confidence.

"You can do it, Zeke!" she called again. Seeing Zeke's cake fall flat on the floor had stirred something in Sharpay. At that moment, she realized that even more than wanting to be on television, she didn't want to see Zeke fail. She pointed to the large clock above his head. "Try again!"

Zeke turned around to view the clock. By some miracle, he still had time to bake another cake. He glanced up at the judges, who all nodded at him.

All the Wildcats had rushed down from the bleachers and were standing near Sharpay and Ryan in the front row. They started chanting, "Try again! Try again!"

"You have time," Zeke heard Brett say. He felt

Brett's hand on his back. The host had gotten up and was now standing next to him, careful not to step in all the chocolate mess.

"Listen to your fans over there," Brett said, motioning to Zeke's cheering squad. "You do have time. Make the most of it." He pointed to the floor. "We'll get someone to clean this up."

Zeke considered Brett's advice and rushed over to his friends. But he stopped short before reaching the front row. He actually didn't even know where to begin to start apologizing. He never should have yelled at his friends or decided to do this on his own.

"I'm really sorry that I lost my temper," Zeke blurted out before any of them could speak. He lowered his head and stared at his chocolate-covered sneakers. "I really could use your help."

When he raised his head, Zeke saw a group of smiling faces. He had to pull himself together. And with his friends, he'd be able to do that.

"Here," Taylor said, stepping forward. She pushed a piece of paper into his hand. "Gabriella and I did some research last night. You've only made this cake with your grandma in Atlanta, right?"

"Yeah," Zeke said, wondering why Taylor was asking him that right now.

Taylor grinned. "Well, did it ever occur to you that New Mexico is at a higher altitude than Georgia?"

Now Zeke was totally confused. What was Taylor talking about?

"We adjusted the recipe for the higher altitude here in New Mexico," Gabriella explained.

Taylor continued. "There's a direct correlation between the higher altitude and lower air pressure, which causes the ingredients to interact differently and requires varying the temperatures and cooking times." She took a deep breath and then went on. "As a result, we recalibrated your recipe to optimize it for our atmospheric conditions."

Jason looked confused. "What is she saying?"

Gabriella stepped forward. "We changed

some measurements in the recipe and figured out the right temperature and cooking time."

"That's why the cake was kind of flat and the icing wasn't right!" Taylor cried, once again loving how science played an important role in everyday life.

"See, it wasn't *all* my fault!" Sharpay cried, clapping her hands together. She jumped up and down and gave Ryan a gentle shove. "I told you that I wasn't the worst *sous*-chef."

"I wouldn't go that far," Taylor said, rolling her eyes. "But the elevation difference definitely does impact baking, especially when it comes to baking a cake and making icing. The good news is Zeke still has time to make another cake—and with our new formula it should be perfect!"

Chad was watching West High put their cake into the oven. He gave Zeke a shove toward the stage. "But you better get back out there fast," he said. "Go bake a cake!"

Zeke gave Taylor and Gabriella hugs. "You are geniuses!"

Taylor and Gabriella blushed. "Thanks," they said at the same time.

"Now where are my *sous*-chefs?" Zeke called, racing back to the kitchen. "Come on, we've got a cake to bake!"

Sharpay's hands flew to her face as her mouth gaped open. "Really?" she cried. "You'll let me help?"

"Come on, Sharpay," Troy said, grabbing her hand and pulling her up onstage. "Zeke needs us, and there's no time to waste."

The three of them got to work. This time, Sharpay listened to everything that Zeke told her to do. She knew the cameras were following her, but she still mixed and stirred as instructed while Zeke prepared his second cake of the day.

Brett took the microphone and started narrating what was happening onstage. Zeke wasn't paying attention to what he was saying. At this point, all he could think about was finishing the cake on time.

Meanwhile, the West High Knights were busy

creating the decorations for their cake. They all seemed to be at odds with one another. Hilary definitely wasn't as chipper as she had been earlier. As they piled up layer after layer, their cake started to lean to one side. If they were going for the leaning Tower of Pisa, they were in good shape. But Zeke doubted that that was their intention.

"Looks like things aren't perfect for West High, either," Troy whispered to Zeke. He nodded toward their competition across the studio. Eli's face was bright red, and he was huffing and puffing. He kept circling their cake, trying to figure out how to straighten it. He started barking orders. A moment later, their whole team was screaming at one another. "Too many cooks in the kitchen?" Troy mused.

"Maybe," Zeke said, glancing over at the other kitchen. He could see them frantically filling the layers with icing and a portion of the mixed berries meant to decorate the top layer in order to prop up the drooping side. "Looks like they have a major structural issue, but we're cutting it really close on time. We are going to have to hustle when this comes out of the oven."

Smiling, Troy bobbed his head. "So it's the last few seconds of the game, and we've got to score before the buzzer—no fouls, no mistakes."

Zeke grinned at his friend. "You got it!" he cried, slapping his hands together.

The rest of the Wildcats were cheering loudly from the sidelines. They were now all standing by the seats in the front row. Everyone was too excited to quietly sit and watch.

Before Zeke poured the batter into the pans, he held up a bottle of chili powder and searched the crowd for Kelsi. When he caught her eye, he gave the bottle a shake. "A little spice for my friends," he called. He sprinkled the seasoning into the bowl.

Kelsi beamed with pride. She was so happy that she had contributed something to the recipe. She clapped and cheered on the East High chefs.

While the cake was baking, Zeke, Troy, and Sharpay mixed the icing using Taylor and Gabriella's new measurements. To Zeke's surprise, he instantly noticed a difference in the texture.

Troy took a box of red candies from his pocket. "Jason gave me these before," he told Zeke, handing him the box. "He was hoping that you could use them to help out with the decorations."

Taking in his hand a few of the candies, Zeke glanced over to see Jason and Chad hooting and hollering for him. He raised the box in the air and shouted, "Wildcats, let me hear your red roar!"

Jason and Chad responded with a loud cheer and smiled. They got the message that Zeke was going to use the candies on the Wildcats' cake.

When the oven buzzer rang, Zeke once again opened the door. He couldn't bear to look inside, so he handed the oven mitts over to Troy. "You take it out," he said.

"It's perfect!" Sharpay cheered as she looked over Troy's shoulder. She then grabbed the other pans from the oven and brought them over to the cooling rack. The layers of the cake had risen, and they smelled delicious!

Quickly, the three chefs gathered all their decorations and set up the layered cake. Then they decorated it with a large Wildcat logo. Just as the audience was counting down the remaining time on the clock, Zeke carried the finished cake to the judges' table. And this time, the cake and the icing held together.

Eli and his team slid their cake—a towering, ten-layered, lemon-and-vanilla-cream cake, topped with mixed berries—onto the table, as well. The Knights looked proud as they stepped away from their dessert. It was a close call for them, too.

The Wildcats' cake may not have been exactly the cake that Zeke set out to make in the first place, but it looked good to him now. The fact that he'd completed this one with the help of his friends was the big difference. He smiled at Troy and Sharpay as the judges called time and surveyed the two finished cakes on their table.

The Wildcats had tried their best. But as Zeke watched the judges pick up their forks, he had to wonder if their best was good enough.

Zeke stood beside Troy and Sharpay, facing the West High team. Everyone was nervous as they watched the judges taste each cake and then jot down some notes on their pads. Zeke felt like he was about to burst. This was the moment he had been waiting for.

CHAPTER NINE

Gabriella and Taylor stood squeezing each other's hands as they waited for the judges to taste the two cakes. "This is the part of the show that is always so hard to watch," Gabriella said. "The moment the contestants are called to the judges' table is when the judges pick at any flaw they can find and question the chef's decision-making and baking skills."

"Yeah," Chad said, leaning in. "It's already

pretty harsh standing around here waiting. I wish we could have a taste of that cake!" From where he stood, the Wildcats' cake looked pretty tasty. And after smelling all of those baking aromas, he was starving!

Gabriella stood on her toes to catch a glimpse of Troy. He was still onstage with Zeke and Sharpay. They were standing around, waiting, just like everyone in the audience. Gabriella had to hand it to Sharpay: she really did come through in the end. And, Gabriella mused, Sharpay fulfilled her wish to be in front of the cameras, after all.

Zeke looked up and waved to Gabriella. She waved back and held up her other hand to show that her fingers were crossed for good luck.

"I'd like another taste of both of the cakes," Liz Warren said. She was in no rush as she tasted each cake and examined each of the designs. She nodded her head and whispered something in Brett's ear. He smiled and then whispered to Jacques Milleux.

Oh, enough with the suspense! Zeke thought. He was pacing around the island on East High's kitchen set.

"You did your best," Troy told him. He kept his eyes on Brett, wondering when he would take the microphone and announce the winner.

Over by the oven, Sharpay had found a perfect place to wait out the decision. She was right in line with the cameras, and a large one was focused just on her. Perfect, she thought as she perched on one of the stools. She smiled and kept winking at the audience she knew was in front of their TVs at home admiring her.

Finally, Brett shook hands with the two other judges and walked to the center of the stage. Once he got there, the whole studio grew quiet. Everyone was anxious to hear what he had to say. "I'd like to have the head chefs from each team come to the judges' table," he said.

"This is it," Zeke said to Troy. "The moment of chocolate truth." He slowly walked toward the table.

Troy ran over to stand with Gabriella. He hoped that the judges would choose East High's cake as the winner. But first, Zeke had to survive the judges' table.

"Eli, your cake was delicious with a good balance of fruit and cream," Jacques Milleux said in his very heavy French accent. "The design was perfect, with style and height."

"But I wondered what happened here at the top," Liz Warren said, pointing out that there were not enough strawberries to fill the highest layer. "Also, it looks like there are more strawberries on this side of the cake."

"Well . . . er . . ." Eli stammered. "We kind of used up our strawberries evening out the cake, so we filled in the top with extra cream."

Brett nodded. "That was quick thinking. I don't think most people would notice that. And I like the cream. Not too sweet and very light. You dressed it up." He took another forkful. "And it's *deeeelicious!*"

Eli smiled and took a deep breath. He looked

relieved that his judging was over and that Brett liked his team's cake.

Gabriella rolled her eyes at the two standard Brett Lawrence lines. Then she crossed her fingers that he might say the same to Zeke.

"Now Zeke, a flop of a cake usually means a flop of a baker," Liz Warren said in her deadpan way. "Such an error in technique is unforgivable."

Zeke lowered his head. There were boos from the crowd.

Liz Warren held her hand up to the audience. "But," she continued, "the fact that you were able to rally and create another whole cake was very impressive."

Raising his head, Zeke nodded and then turned back to see his friends all standing together. He knew that he never would have been able to do it without them.

"Though you did sacrifice some decoration on the cake," Jacques Milleux added. Then he smiled. "But the cake was moist and delicious. I liked the spice in it, as well."

A smile spread across Zeke's face. He was so glad that he had made the second cake. And Kelsi beamed with pride.

"I love the red candies," Brett said. "They dressed it up!" He dug his fork into the cake again. "And I agree with Jacques. The spice makes the cake *deeeelicious*!"

Hearing those refrains now made Gabriella laugh and cheer along with all the other Wildcats.

"Zeke, Zeke, he's our man. He's our baker; we're his fans!" all the Wildcats sang out.

A little embarrassed, Zeke waved at his cheering section. Then he turned back to hear the final verdict of the cake competition.

"It was a very hard decision for me, and for the judges," Brett told the two chefs. "But we have selected the winner of this challenge." He stood up and took the official *Bake-Off* trophy from the table and held it up so that everyone could see. "But first we'd like to thank both schools and their principals for making this challenge possible. We've had a great time here today, and we hope to see you all back in the kitchen again soon."

The audience applauded, and Brett had to quiet the crowd before he continued. "And now for the winner! We give this trophy to West High for their deliciously light and flavorful lemon-and-vanilla-cream layered cake!"

The Knights screamed and jumped around, while the Wildcats politely clapped for their rivals. Zeke shook all three of the judges' hands and then shook Eli's hand before he escaped off the stage. He wanted to get away from the bright lights and cameras. He wanted to run and hide.

Before he got very far, though, he heard a familiar voice. "Wait," Brett said to him. "I have more to say to you."

Yeah, Zeke thought. He wants to tell me that I am terrible in the kitchen and that I shouldn't have been the head chef. Zeke looked down at his feet. He slumped his shoulders.

"Listen," Brett went on. "What you and your friends did out there was amazing! I really didn't think that you could come from behind and get the job done. But you did." Brett smiled and paused until Zeke looked up at him. "You can take the heat, and that is a very important quality in a chef."

Zeke was starting to feel a little bit better. He stood up straighter and looked Brett in the eyes. "Thanks," he said.

"And you have quite a team out there," Brett said, laughing. "Working in a busy restaurant kitchen can be chaotic and being able to manage the team is very important. I hear that you are a basketball star, too. I guess that's where you learned about teamwork, huh?"

"Something like that," Zeke said. But the team that helped him win was more than his basketball team; they were his friends. And they were the best team around. Suddenly, it wasn't such a big deal that West High won the trophy. Zeke knew that he had friends who were there for him, no matter what. And that was the greatest prize of all.

"Thanks, Brett," Zeke said. "This has really meant a lot to me."

"I'm glad," Brett told him. "Now we have a wrap party with a lot of cake to eat!" He gave Zeke a wink and went back to the stage. Zeke watched him as he shook hands and signed autographs. One day, he might be a celebrity chef like Brett Lawrence, but most important, he'd always have his friends by his side.

CHAPTER
TEN

The house lights came up, and the studio quickly turned into a large party space. The two kitchen sets were rolled off to the side to make a wide dance floor and eating area. Both West High and East High were ready to party—and eat cake!

Brett Lawrence and the two other judges mingled with the crowd for a while, talking and signing autographs. Zeke was surprised to see how many students followed Brett's show, or read Liz's reviews, or had actually dined at La Mer. The rest of the students lined up for cake or headed out to the center of the dance floor. Everyone enjoyed having a taste of the two cakes and listening to the music from the DJ spinning in the corner.

The West High team had taken off their matching aprons, but most of them left on their Knights chef hats. They spilled onto the dance floor for a celebratory dance. Hilary tapped Sharpay on her shoulder, ready to gloat. "Great competition, huh?" she said.

Sharpay gave Hilary a long look. The only disappointment of her day was not being able to enjoy beating Hilary again. She was about to say something to her, but Ryan pulled on her hand. Through gritted teeth, Ryan coached his sister, hoping to avoid a big scene. "Just say congratulations," he whispered.

Sharpay did as directed, flashing a quick smile at Hilary. "Congratulations," she said flatly. You win some and you lose some, she thought. But then, before turning away, she couldn't help herself. "Oh, by the way, you have some berry seeds in your teeth," she said. "You might want to clean up before you talk to anyone else." Sharpay tossed her blond hair as she headed over to a circle of West High guys who had been smiling at her during the judging and were now motioning her to come over. Hilary might have won this round, but she certainly hadn't won it all. As far as Sharpay was concerned, this was a victory for her, too. After all, she was now legitimately a television star.

Principal Matsui and Ms. Davis rushed over to Zeke. They were both excited to congratulate him. "Well done," the principal said, placing his hand on Zeke's shoulder. "That was a great effort out there! And you really showed your fellow Wildcats what it means to not give up. I'm really proud of you, Zeke." He pointed to the plate full of chocolate cake in his hand. "And this is quite a cake. I don't think I could have made the decision between the two. They are both out-standing."

Ms. Davis gave Zeke a hug. "You're a fantastic head chef!" she burst out. "I knew that we picked the right person for the job. You gave this your best effort. Thank you." She gave Zeke another squeeze. "And I love this cake!" She put a forkful of chocolate cake in her mouth.

Zeke was practically glowing. He thanked them—though he knew there was one person he *really* had to thank. He searched the crowd until he found the Wildcat he was looking for.

Enjoying her circle of admiring fans, Sharpay chatted with the guys from West High. She was smiling and bobbing her head as they all vied for her attention. Zeke walked over and reached into the group, gently pulling Sharpay away.

"Listen, Sharpay," he said. "I need to tell you how much I appreciated your support today. It meant a lot to me."

Sharpay smiled and took a bite of the cake that she was holding. "Sure," she said, giving a wink to one of the guys watching her. "It was really fun."

"And you were on television, so you got the only thing *you* truly wanted," Zeke added.

Trying not to look shocked that Zeke could say such a thing, Sharpay just stood there staring at him. Now he had her complete attention, since he obviously knew her plan all along.

Pleased that he had captured her interest, Zeke continued before she could say anything. "I know you offered to be my *sous*-chef because you wanted to be on TV," he said matter-of-factly. He could tell that Sharpay was about to protest, so he jumped in again. "That's cool. I get it. You love the spotlight." He smiled at her and then went on. "But I want you to know that you really helped me with this, and I really appreciated you being there. Especially after the way I kind of blew up the other day. Without your support today, I would never have been able to make the second cake."

"Well, good," Sharpay said, a bit flustered.

She wasn't exactly prepared for Zeke to say all that to her. She couldn't believe that he had seen through her plan all along. Actually, she thought that he still might be angry at her for messing up the recipe in the first place. Feeling a bit uncomfortable, she took another bite of cake. With her mouth full of chocolate, she casually tried to change the subject. "This cake is *soooo* good."

Zeke shrugged. "I couldn't have done it without all the help from my friends. We were a great team today. Thank you."

His sincerity got her, and Sharpay leaned in closer to him. "You know, you really are a good chef," she whispered. "Those pastries that you made this week were the best I've ever tasted." She turned her head toward Jacques Milleux. "And that includes the pastries at La Mer." Tossing her head from side to side, she returned to her circle of admirers.

"Thanks," Zeke said as he watched her walk away. The grin on his face felt as if it would be stuck there for a week.

Just then, Chad, Jason, and Kelsi pounced on him.

"Zeke, you were awesome!" Kelsi exclaimed, glowing with joy for her friend.

"Yeah, you didn't get the trophy, but that cake is the chocolate champion!" Chad said enthusiastically. Then he waved his arm, gesturing at the roomful of people having a good time. "And this party rocks!"

"I don't know about you," Jason said, "but I am ready for slice number two." He nodded at Kelsi, inviting her to come along, and the two of them took off to get another piece. They ran right into Gabriella and Troy.

"Slow down. We're not on the court," Troy said to Jason, laughing.

Gabriella giggled. She knew that Jason's motivation for getting more cake was almost as intense as his drive to win on the basketball court. She couldn't blame him—the cake was delicious!

"Zeke couldn't have done it without you and

Taylor," Troy said to Gabriella as Jason and Kelsi got in line for their second piece of cake. "Those measurements meant everything. How'd you think of that?"

Gabriella shrugged. "Taylor and I were talking about Sharpay's mistake and wondering if that was the only cause of the first cake disaster."

"Huh," Troy said, still amazed. "Great call!"

"Thanks," Gabriella replied. She was feeling pretty happy about what she and Taylor had discovered. "And you were great as a *sous*-chef. I didn't think you knew the first thing about baking."

Taking her hand, Troy led Gabriella toward the dance floor. "I don't," Troy confessed. "Zeke asked me to be his second *sous*-chef just so I could divert Sharpay," he whispered. "She was driving him crazy with her costume changes and television-camera obsession. I was just supposed to keep her occupied so he could concentrate on cooking. But I guess he really did need us both in the end."

"Yeah," Gabriella said with a laugh. "But you should've known that no one can control Sharpay Evans."

"That's for sure," Troy said. "But she did come through for Zeke today. She was a big part of motivating him to make that second cake."

Gabriella had to agree. And she was glad. It was really nice to see Sharpay cheer Zeke on. It was more than fair payback for all the attention and pastries that he had given her.

Gabriella and Troy reached the dance floor and started to groove. Chad and Taylor were already there, and so were Kelsi and Jason—after finishing their scrumptious second helpings. Ryan and Sharpay were doing a complicated line dance and getting everyone on the floor involved. East High and West High students were all blending together and having a great time.

Zeke danced over to Gabriella and Troy, grinning. "Thanks again," he said as he moved to the pulsing beat of the song. "You're both the best."

He took his cell phone out of his pocket. "And now I gotta call Grandma Emma. I have to tell her about some new additions to the family chocolate recipe, New Mexico–style!"

"You mean Wildcat-style!" Taylor shouted.

All Zeke's friends cheered. Even though West High had the trophy, East High had a winning team. And that was something to celebrate.

Something new is on the way!
Look for the next book in the High School
Musical: Stories from East High series. . . .

IN THE SPOTLIGHT

By Catherine Hapka
Based on the Disney Channel Original Movie
"High School Musical," Written by Peter Barsocchini
Based on "High School Musical 2," Written by Peter Barsocchini
Based on Characters Created by Peter Barsocchini

"Go wide, Bolton!" Chad Danforth cried, dribbling his basketball down the school hallway.

Troy Bolton grinned at his best friend. It was Friday morning before homeroom, and the halls of East High were crowded with students. "I'm open!" he called. Troy dodged a passing

104

sophomore and lifted both hands over his head.

Chad whizzed the ball toward him. Another teammate, Jason Cross, leaped for the interception, but Troy caught the ball easily. He dribbled around Jason and threw it to Zeke Baylor.

"Can't you give it a rest already?" shouted a loud voice. "You guys can play basketball while we're off from school next week. Do you have to turn the hallway into an obstacle course, too?"

Troy turned and saw that Taylor McKessie, Martha Cox, Kelsi Nielsen, and Gabriella Montez had just appeared around the corner. Taylor, who had just yelled at them, had her arms crossed over her chest and her lips pursed as she glared at the guys—especially Chad. Taylor was an excellent student and took school very seriously. She didn't have much patience for people who didn't feel the same way, although she'd loosened up a little bit since getting to know Chad better. Still, though deep down she really liked Chad, she thought he could be very immature sometimes.

While Chad tried to defend their ball playing, Troy and Gabriella looked at one another and smiled. Troy thought Gabriella was the most most amazing girl he'd ever met. Luckily for him, she thought he was just as special. The two of them had been an item ever since they'd co-starred in the school's winter musical the previous year.

"Hey," he said, stepping toward her.

"Hey, yourself," Gabriella said, her brown eyes sparkling. "And Taylor's right. Thanks to those teacher conferences and emergency school repairs to the roof, you'll have four whole days next week to play basketball from morning to night."

"Too bad they didn't just give us the whole week off," Chad complained. He dribbled the ball around himself in a circle. "I mean, what's the point of making us come in on Monday when we're off for the rest of the week? What if we wanted to take the time to go somewhere on vacation or something?"

"Yeah, right." Jason snorted and reached out to steal the ball. "Were you planning to use your allowance to jet off to Tibet for some mountain climbing?"

"Nah. Tibet's not really my style." Chad grinned and snatched the ball back. "I was thinking more like windsurfing in Jamaica." He spun the ball around and shot it at the girls. "Think fast, Gabriella!"

"Oh!" Gabriella hadn't been expecting the pass. She grabbed for the ball, but it bounced off her fingertips and bonked Kelsi in the shoulder. "Oops! I'm so sorry, Kelsi!" Gabriella cried, her cheeks turning pink.

"Uh-oh! Butterfingers!" Chad cried with a laugh.

"Good thing there weren't any NBA scouts around, Gabriella," Zeke teased.

"Yeah. You'd never get a contract with the Lakers if they saw that fumble," Jason added, giving her a kind smile.

Gabriella rolled her eyes and smiled back.

"That's fine. I'm holding out for a deal with the Celtics anyway," she joked.

"That a girl!" Martha called.

Kelsi laughed as Martha retrieved the ball from the floor and tossed it to Chad, who caught it easily and spun it on one finger.

Troy grabbed it from him. "Leave her alone, guys," he said with a slight frown. "Gabriella might not be Shaq, but not everyone has to be an athlete. She has plenty of other talents."

"Thanks, Troy," Gabriella said. Still, she couldn't help being a tiny bit insulted. Not an athlete? All she had done was miss one pass. She wasn't *that* clumsy! But she didn't say anything. After all, she knew that Troy meant well.

Besides, she was distracted by a commotion at the far end of the hall. Sharpay Evans was coming around the corner with her twin brother, Ryan. Sharpay liked to create a scene wherever she went, but she seemed particularly loud today.

The others noticed, too. "What's with Sharpay?" Jason wondered.

Chad shrugged. "Noisy . . . a crowd following her . . . looks like business as usual to me," he commented.

Gabriella sighed. Sharpay was an experienced actress and the co-president of East High's Drama Club (along with Ryan, of course). But playing the lead role in almost every play or musical wasn't enough for her. She was the kind of person who always acted as if she were performing onstage, even if she was just walking down the hall.

As Sharpay drew closer, Gabriella and her friends could hear what she was saying. In fact, it was hard not to hear it. Ms. Darbus, the head of the Drama Club, always liked to tell her young actors to "project, project, PROJECT!" Sharpay had a talent for projecting.

". . . and so now Daddy is flying the whole family out to L.A. for the premiere," Sharpay was saying to the small but adoring crowd gathered around her. "It's going to be fabulous. We'll probably spend the whole week at our beach house in Malibu—I'm sure half of Hollywood will want to stop by and congratulate us. Not just anyone will be invited to the big night, you know."

"That's right!" Ryan added eagerly. "It's going to be *very* exclusive."

Gabriella couldn't help being curious. "Hi, guys," she said, stepping toward Sharpay and Ryan. "What's going on?"

Chad visibly winced. "Ooh, now she's done it," he muttered, clutching his basketball in both hands. "We're actually going to have to hear about it!"

Sharpay ignored him, even though his comment had been loud enough for her to hear. "Well, I suppose *everyone* will know soon," she told Gabriella. "You may have already heard that my father helped fund a very prestigious indie film this year."

As a matter-of-fact, Gabriella *hadn't* heard that. Judging by the looks on her friends' faces, neither had they. But it didn't matter. Sharpay didn't wait for a response.

"It's called *Angst in Altoona,* and it's had a lot of prerelease buzz," she said. "In the industry, that's what we say when people are saying positive things about your film before it premieres."

"We?" Chad echoed, raising one eyebrow at Troy and Taylor. Troy grinned and shrugged, and Taylor just snorted.

"*Angst in Altoona*?" Zeke wrinkled his nose, looking confused.

"Sounds kind of, um, unusual," Martha added.

"Is that Altoona, Pennsylvania? Because they have a minor league baseball team—the Curve," Jason said. He knew just about everything there was to know about sports. "Is the movie about baseball?"

"Oh, that'd be cool!" Suddenly, Chad looked a lot more interested. "If it is, can your dad get us free tickets, Sharpay?"

Sharpay rolled her eyes upward. "First of all, it's definitely *not* about baseball," she huffed. "And even if it was, it's not like it's going to be playing at the multiplex down at the mall. This is an *art* film."

"But tell them the best part!" Ryan broke in, practically jumping up and down.

"I'm getting there." Sharpay patted her flawless blond hair. "Daddy is so pleased with all this that he's flying the whole family out to L.A. for the premiere. We'll be staying all week, rubbing elbows with the rich and famous. Isn't that fabulous?"

The gang exchanged surprised looks. This was big news!

Sharpay's upcoming trip to L.A. was the talk of East High for the rest of the day. It wasn't often that someone from East High traveled to Hollywood.

"It stinks," Chad grumbled, dribbling his basketball down the hall as he and Troy headed for their lockers after last period. Sharpay was just ahead of them, walking in the center of a little circle of admirers. "Here I was all psyched about having four days off from school," Chad continued. "And now all I'll be able to think about is how Sharpay and Ryan are spending the week living it up celeb-style!"

"Aw, come on," Troy said. "Honestly, would you want to be going to some Hollywood film premiere? I mean, they'd probably make you wear a suit or something."

Chad scowled. "Hey, bro, for a week living the life in Cali, I'd put on two suits."

There was no basketball practice that day, so Troy and Chad headed outside after a quick stop at their lockers. Zeke and Jason were already hanging out on the steps with Martha, Taylor, and Kelsi. Chad joined them, while Troy looked around for Gabriella. He wanted to ask her what she had planned for their days off next week. Even though he'd definitely be playing basketball every day, he also wanted to make plans with Gabriella.

He spotted her at the bottom of the steps. "Hi," he said, hurrying over.

"Hi," she replied with a smile.

Before either of them could say anything else, a sleek black sports car pulled up to the curb. The driver honked its loud horn.

Gabriella shaded her eyes and squinted. "Isn't that Sharpay's dad's car?"

"Uh-huh," Troy said. He and most of his friends had spent the previous summer working at the nearby Lava Springs Country Club, which meant he'd seen Mr. and Mrs. Evans pull up in that car more times than he could count.

The door of the black car opened, and Mr. Evans got out. He was a handsome, confident-looking man. He was wearing a fancy suit and well-polished shoes. He gave the group a friendly wave and started to walk over to them.

"Troy Bolton!" Mr. Evans called out in his jovial voice. His white teeth gleamed brightly. "And is that the lovely Gabriella? Nice to see you kids again."

"You too, sir," Troy said with a smile. Sharpay's father had taken a special interest in him over the summer. He had introduced Troy to some very important people who could help him get on a college basketball team. While that had caused Troy a few problems at the time, he had still appreciated it.

"I hear congratulations are in order," Troy said to Mr. Evans. "Sharpay says your film is going to be a big hit."

Mr. Evans chuckled. "Let's hope so, son," he said. "I didn't get into this venture expecting to make much money, but hey—if it happens, I won't complain!"

At that moment, Sharpay hurried over, with Ryan right at her heels. "What are you doing here, Daddy?" she demanded. "I thought Mother was picking us up and taking us shopping for outfits for the premiere."

"She got held up at her yoga class, princess," Mr. Evans said, checking his watch. "I'm going to drop you kids off at the boutique on my way to the office, and she'll join you there in a little while."

Troy and Gabriella's friends had all drifted over to them by now. "That movie premiere sounds awesome, sir," Zeke spoke up.

"Oh, it should be a good time," Mr. Evans agreed. Just then, his eyes lit up. "Say, that gives me a terrific idea. Why don't you all come along?"

"All?" Sharpay repeated in horror.

"You mean to the movie premiere?" Taylor exclaimed.

"In California?" added Kelsi.

"Really?" Zeke gasped.

"Do we have to wear a suit?" asked Chad.

"You can wear whatever you like!" Mr. Evans slung an arm around Troy's shoulders and beamed at all of them. "The more the merrier, eh gang? There's plenty of room at our beach house, and I have more frequent flier miles than I could ever possibly use, and heck, it's my movie—I should certainly be able to score a few extra passes for the premiere. So what do you say?"

"What do we say?" Chad responded for all of them with a grin, pumping his fist in the air. "We say we're going to *Hollywood*!"

HIGH SCHOOL MUSICAL

CAN'T GET ENOUGH HIGH SCHOOL MUSICAL?

The *Stories from East High* series are original stories based on your favorite Wildcats!

Available wherever books are sold

© Disney

DISNEP PRESS

www.disneybooks.com

The must-have book for any fan of *High School Musical!*

SECRET PASSWORD FOR AN EXCLUSIVE WEB PAGE AND **HIGH SCHOOL MUSICAL 3** DOWNLOADS INSIDE!

Experience the world of East High like never before with this complete behind-the-scenes guide to *High School Musical*, *High School Musical 2*, and now an UPDATED web page with *High School Musical 3* content!

With lots of removable extras!